KU-273-392

GLO Friends™
GLO Butterfly's magic

written by JUNE WOODMAN
illustrated by CAROLE THOMPSON

Ladybird Books

Quite hidden, deep inside the woods,
The world of Glo Land lies.
Its houses, decked with plants and flowers,
Are safe from prying eyes.

Glo Butterfly lives happily
With all her Glo Land friends.
She's pretty and so graceful, as
She swoops and twirls and bends.

The Glo Friends live in a magical place called Glo Land. This colourful rhyming story tells of one of their adventures.

British Library Cataloguing in Publication Data
Woodman, June
    Glo Butterfly.—(Glo friends; 2)
    I. Title   II. Thompson, Carole   III. Series
    823'.914[J]   PZ7
    ISBN 0-7214-0975-X

First edition

Published by Ladybird Books Ltd Loughborough Leicestershire UK
Ladybird Books Inc Lewiston Maine 04240 USA

Her wand is always close to hand
Throughout both day and night;
She thinks it can work magic spells –
Which isn't always right.

It never seems to bother her
As she floats on her way,
That broken things *stay* broken, she
Just tries again next day.

One morning Glo Grannybug
Breaks her best pot in two.
"Don't worry," says Glo Butterfly.
"I'll make it good as new!"

She wildly waves her wand about
And hums her magic song.
Glo Grannybug says, "Oh dear me!
Your magic spell's gone wrong."

Glo Butterfly is sure that soon
Those two halves will be one.
She gaily flutters off to see
Who else needs magic done.

Poor Glo Snail's looking gloomy, for
His fence has fallen down.
Glo Butterfly says, "I've a spell.
You do not need to frown."

She waves her wand so madly that
It makes a chilly breeze.
Sad Glo Snail groans, "My fence is still
Down flat," and starts to sneeze.

Quite undisturbed, Glo Butterfly
Flies swiftly off to see
Glo Spider in her tiny house.
She says, "Come in for tea."

But when Glo Butterfly sits down
In Glo Spider's arm-chair,
One leg breaks and Glo Butterfly's
Neat feet wave in the air.

Poor Glo Spider is overcome
As Glo Butterfly falls flat.
"I'll magic it back on," she says.
"There is no doubt of that."

Again she flourishes her wand,
But carelessly she hits
Glo Spider's lovely lampshade, and
It breaks in little bits.

They scramble on their hands and knees
To pick the pieces up.
Glo Butterfly sits down to tea,
And drops a favourite cup!

Glo Spider says, "I really think
It's time you went away.
You've broken *far* too many of
My lovely things today."

Glo Spider says that Glo Friends know
Glo Butterfly's great spells
Have *never* really worked at all.
(The truth she *always* tells.)

Glo Butterfly picks up her wand
And sadly says goodbye.
While trailing homewards on her own,
A tear drops from her eye.

As she goes on, Glo Bug pops out
To ask if she will make
A spell to fix the handle back
Upon his garden rake.

"Oh bother your old rake!" she cries.
"You're teasing me, I know.
I'm no good at this magic game.
Glo Spider told me so."

Down by the Glo Pond young Glo Worm
Is looking at the swing.
When Glo Butterfly walks sadly past
He says, "The very thing!

This seat is broken. Can you help
And sing your magic rhyme?
Just wave your wand – I know that you
Can mend it in no time!"

To his surprise, Glo Butterfly
Sinks down in floods of tears.
There must be something *very* wrong
With her, he greatly fears.

In great distress she tells him that
Her magic all goes wrong,
In spite of such a pretty wand
And quite a clever song.

"I'll tell you something," Glo Worm says,
"If I'm upset like you,
I go and see Glo Grannybug.
She knows just what to do."

"You're right!" Glo Butterfly declares.
"Glo Grannybug is wise."
She tucks her wand under her arm
And quickly wipes her eyes.

Together, she and Glo Worm go
Up to the garden gate.
"Perhaps I shouldn't bother her,"
She says. "It's getting late."

But Glo Worm pushes her inside
And tells her with a grin,
"It's not too late for good advice.
Just knock, and go on in."

"Come in, dear," beams Glo Grannybug,
"I'm busy, as you see;
I'm brewing up my super glue.
It's sticky as can be."

"I'm so sad," says Glo Butterfly,
"My magic's gone away."
"What nonsense," says Glo Grannybug.
"Why, *magic's* here to stay.

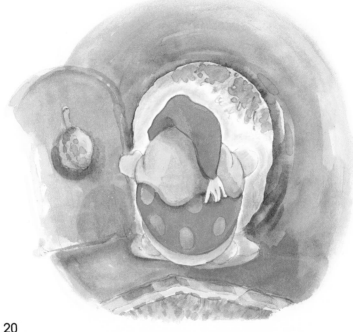

"There's magic in a rainbow bright,
Or rose-buds fresh with dew,
In home-made jams, and new-born lambs,
And in my super glue!

21

"I always say the harder that
We work and think each day,
The more things seem quite magical,
In every kind of way."

Glo Butterfly thinks *very* hard,
Then tiptoes out that night
With lots of sticky super glue –
Now, she can put things right.

She sticks Glo Snail's fence up again,
And then, all of a quake,
She searches the dark garden till
She finds young Glo Bug's rake.

She mends Glo Spider's broken chair,
And then she glues the cup.
She makes a lamp-shade jig-saw with
The pieces they picked up.

Then down beside the Glo Pond she
Quite swiftly mends the swing.
"I think that is the lot," she sighs,
"I've mended everything."

Next day she wakes up *very* late,
But then thinks, "*I forgot*!
The one thing that I should have done,
Was Glo Grannybug's best pot."

Then someone rings at her front door
And voices call, "Hello!
It's picnic time by Glo Pond, and
We're starting now, you know."

Oh, what a super sight she sees.
She greets it with a cry.
Such piles and piles of pizzas, in
Glo Grannybug's pot stacked high!

Glo Grannybug sees her surprise
And winks one twinkly eye.
"It's **magic** here in Glo Land,"
Smiles happy Glo Butterfly.